NEW HAVEN PUBLIC
NEW HAVEN FREE PUBLIC LIBRARY
3 5000 09501 6696
P9-CFW-377

THUNDERBIRD
and Other Stories

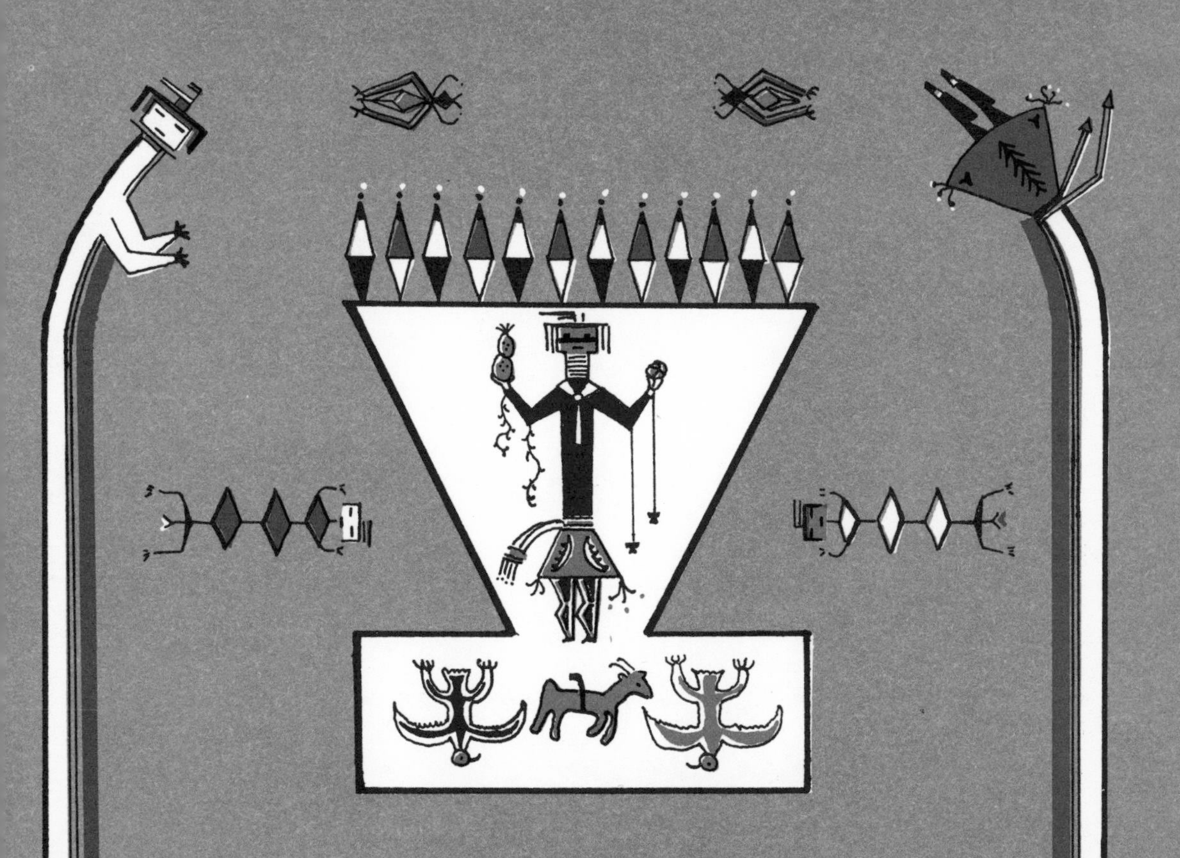

THUNDERBIRD and Other Stories

Henry Chafetz

Illustrations by Ronni Solbert

Pantheon

To the children, not born yet, of my sons, Michael and Eric. They also shall know these stories.

This title was originally catalogued by the Library of Congress as follows:

Chafetz, Henry.
Thunderbird, and other stories. Illus. by Ronni Solbert.
[New York] Pantheon [1964]

41 p. col. illus. 27 cm.

Three legends of the American Indians, retold by the author.

CONTENTS.—Thunderbird.—The tale of Bat.—The peace pipe.

1. Indians of North America—Legends—Juvenile literature.
I. Title.

E98.F6C47 j 398.2 64-18317

Library of Congress [3]

Trade Ed.: ISBN: 0-394-81747-8 Lib. Ed.: ISBN: 0-394-91747-2

 Published in New York by Pantheon Books, a division of Random House, Inc., and simultaneously in Toronto, Canada, by Random House of Canada, Limited. Manufactured in the United States of America.

Contents

THUNDERBIRD
and Other Stories

Thunderbird

When the earth was new, giants lived among the Indians. And the greatest of the giants that then walked the earth was Nasan. One hundred feet high Nasan stood, and each step he took was a mile long. Five feet wide was the space between his eyes, and his mouth when it was open seemed as large as a valley. His teeth looked like stumps of bright white birch trees when he smiled.

Nasan's dwelling place was at one end of the earth on a very high mountain facing the Eastern Ocean, and his lodge was on the tallest peak of this mountain where the blue clouds met and passed each other. Nasan lived here all alone. He was a lonely giant.

One night, around the council fire of the giants, it was agreed that the Evening Star Lady was the fairest of all the women known to the great ones of the world. The Evening Star was lovely and bright to see, rising and shining in the sky each night.

The Indians respected and feared all the great beings — the Great Spirit, all the animal gods, all the bird gods, and the giants also — but they loved the Evening Star Lady.

She was many things to the Indians. Each night the calendar men of the tribes looked to the rising of the Evening Star as the time to make another cut in their calendar sticks. The wanderer, the war scout, and the hunter returning home late at night always looked forward to the Evening Star to guide them on the trail. And to her only, the young Indian lovers sang happy songs and told the secrets in their hearts.

Now, Nasan was lonely.

"A pity it is," he said to himself, "that I have no wife to mend my moccasins, to keep my lodge in order, and to cook for me."

The giant looked up in the sky at the Evening Star Lady. His heart leaped with delight as he beheld her brightness, and at once he knew he had a great love for her. Nasan was determined to have the Evening Star Lady for his wife.

The giant called for the old Needlewoman.

Out of the cave where she made her home came the one-eyed Needlewoman. She came with her witching needles, her magic loom, and her buckskin bag of medicine.

"Make me wings, Grandmother," Nasan said to the Needlewoman. "I wish to go on a journey to the sky."

The Needlewoman was very old. Her hair was white and

her one good eye was gray and deep. Old she was, but her hands were quick-moving and her fingers nimble.

In mid-forest by the light of the moon, while animal and Indian slept, the Needlewoman made the wings.

She took one thousand feathers from one hundred wild birds, and she obtained the finest and strongest thread from the gray spiders who lived in the shadowy places of the Gloomy Hills where the mists linger. The Needlewoman stitched and hitched, and with the thread she bound the feathers together.

She deftly wove the silver of the moonbeams, the breath of a fleet deer, and the speed of a darting arrow into the wings.

The Needlewoman made a paint from the bark of a hemlock tree, and she colored the wings red.

She then dipped the wings in the waters of the Great Lake of Salt, and thus she made the wings strong.

Then the Needlewoman called for Nasan. Only a giant could carry these large and strong wings on his back. But Nasan was the greatest of the giants, and the wings fit him well.

Nasan soared like a big bird right up to the Evening Star Lady.

He brought her a buckskin bead bag and many white shells, and he dropped ermine skins and buffalo robes at her feet. Nasan promised the Evening Star Lady he would do anything she ever wished, if she would make her home in his lodge.

The Evening Star Lady smiled at the giant and put her arms around him. Off he flew with her to his mountain home.

The next night the Evening Star Lady did not appear in the sky. The night was gloomy.

The Indians looked and looked, but the Evening Star no longer shone in the sky at night. The night wanderers became lost, the calendar men could not keep the right time, and worst of all, the Indian lovers were dejected. Gone were their dreams, gone were their sweet songs, for gone was the Evening Star Lady, their star of love.

There was much sorrow among all the Indians. They assembled from near and far and cried out to the Great Spirit, who was the ruler of the sky:

"O Great Mystery, find and bring back for us the Evening Star Lady."

The Great Spirit looked over the edge of the sky and heard the cries of the Indians. The Great Spirit looked into his know-it-all medicine bag and saw that the Evening Star Lady had flown off with Nasan the giant.

The Great Spirit ordered Nasan to let the Evening Star Lady return to her place in the sky. But Nasan refused to give her up.

Now the Great Spirit was angry.

This was not good.

He swore an almighty oath to punish the giant.

The Great Spirit rattled his great war drum:

BOOM! BOOM! BOOM!

The Great Spirit sounded his war cry:

HI YI! HI YI! HI YI! YI! YI!

Now Nasan, being a giant, was also a wizard who knew mighty magic.

When he heard the Great Spirit's war cry, Nasan pulled up a tall pine tree out of the ground. He used the tree, as he would a pencil, to draw a circle around his lodge. Four times he drew a ring around his home, and by placing a strong charm over the inside of the circle, made it a magic zone where no harm could come to him.

The Great Spirit rode the winds to the mountain home of

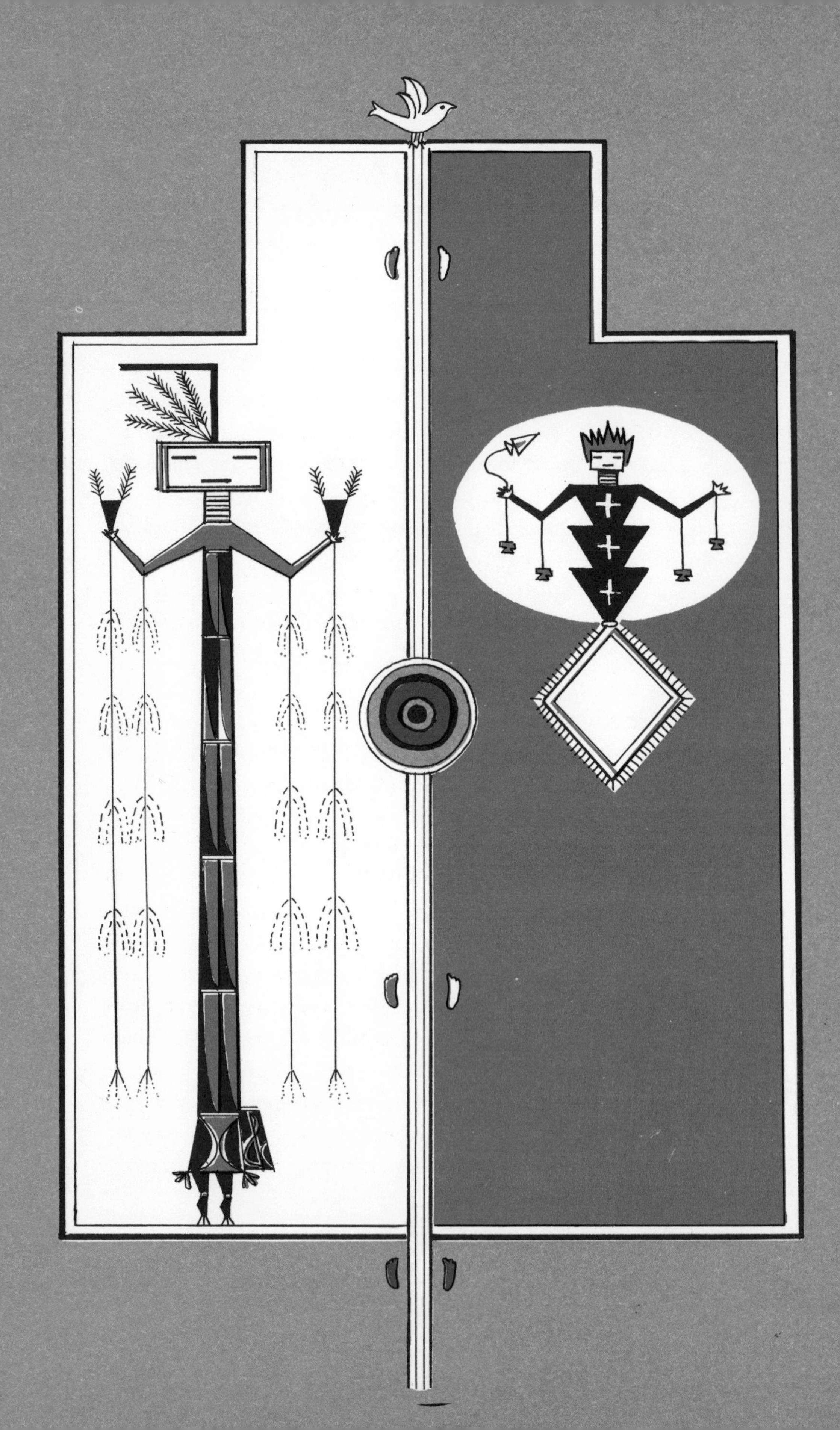

Nasan. With his hands he shook the mountain.

The grass flew and many trees fell as the mountain rocked. But the grass within the magic ring all around Nasan's lodge stood still, the trees were unshaken, and the giant's lodge did not fall.

The Great Spirit breathed upon the mountain.

His breath was fierce and burning, and out of it there came a roaring of fire and smoke that swept over the mountain, scorching all the land before it. But the fire crumbled to cold ashes at the edge of Nasan's charmed circle.

Truly, there was strong medicine in the giant's magic.

The Great Spirit sent five hundred dark shapes and weird forms to the home of Nasan. They could go no further than the outside of the circle. The Great Spirit sent cold and he sent floods. But these also failed to cross the edge of the ring. It was like a strong wall; nothing could pass it.

Now the Great Spirit, who knew everything, knew that the Evening Star Lady desired above all things a robe of white deerskin. Through the Evening Star Lady, then, he would lure Nasan out from the protection of the magic circle.

The Great Spirit went to the Chief of the Ants and instructed him what to do and say.

The Chief of the Ants took his people to the mountain where Nasan lived, and the ants began to eat holes in the mountain. They dug and dug their way upwards until they came right underneath the floor of Nasan's lodge.

That night, as Nasan and the Evening Star Lady lay down to sleep, they heard voices beneath them. The giant and the Evening Star Lady, like all the great beings, knew the languages of all creatures — whether human, bird, animal, or insect. Nasan and the Evening Star Lady put their ears to the earth floor of the lodge and the words of the ants reached them from the ground underneath their sleeping blankets.

"One must see this wondrous white deer for himself," said an ant.

"Is it really all white?" another ant asked.

"Whiter than snow, silver, or clouds. White beyond all belief is this deer."

The ants talked in very loud voices to make certain that Nasan and the Evening Star Lady would hear.

"Where does this more than snow-white deer live?" asked one ant.

"This astounding white deer runs wild and free in the nearby forest of the hemlock trees."

"Surely," another ant said, "it is the only white deer in the world."

The Evening Star Lady could not sleep that night knowing there was a white deer near by, and during the day she could not rest for thinking about the beautiful white robe its skin would make for her. The Evening Star Lady felt she could not live without such a robe.

"Husband," she said to Nasan, "I am most anxious for a white deerskin robe."

So great was Nasan's love for the Evening Star Lady, and so strong was her wish, that he agreed to go on a hunt for the white deer.

The giant set out down the mountain for the forest of the hemlock trees. He moved cautiously, knowing the Great Spirit was still on the warpath against him.

The Great Spirit, who was hiding behind a gray cloud in the sky, watched Nasan leave his lodge. The Great Spirit was pleased that his plan had succeeded. He knew that no amount of caution could save Nasan from him once the giant left the protection of the charmed circle.

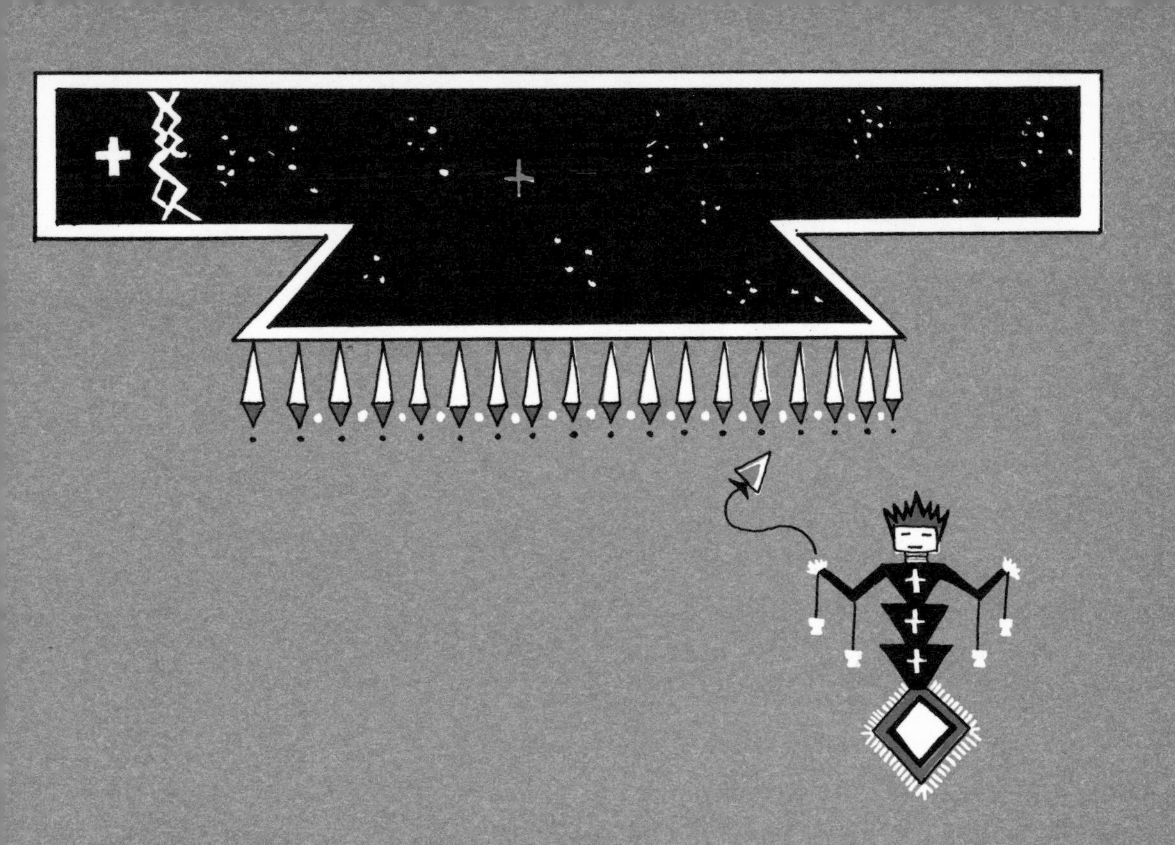

The moment Nasan stepped across the magic circle, the Great Spirit came out of his hiding place in the sky and seized him. With ten thousand phantom hands the Great Spirit held Nasan. Sharper than spears were the Great Spirit's fingers. Stronger than the bull moose, stronger even than the oak tree, were his hands.

With a roar that echoed across the earth, Nasan tried to break away, but the Great Spirit's hands held the giant on all sides. Like ten thousand hammers the fists of the Great Spirit beat pain against Nasan's bones.

Each way the giant turned and fought, he was beaten back by the phantom hands.

Nasan clutched at the hands he could not see and grappled fiercely with them. But for every hand he tore away from his body, ten more seized him.

The shouts of the Great Spirit and the giant were fearsome to hear, and the earth shook as they struggled with each other.

The fight continued from mountain to plain. Four suns, four moons, the Great Spirit and Nasan the giant fought each other.

Nasan crashed over mountains and staggered backwards into the great broad rivers. The Great Spirit marveled at Nasan's strength. Truly, he was the mightiest of giants.

But the giant fell to the earth at last, exhausted and beaten. The ground shook and crumbled and became a valley where he fell.

Thus, the Great Spirit captured Nasan and pulled him up to the sky.

The Great Spirit was not cruel or wicked, and he admired those who battled bravely and well. The giant, however, had disobeyed the Great Spirit's command, and brave or not, he must be punished.

The Great Spirit changed the giant into a large and awesome eagle.

"Your name shall be Thunderbird, ruler of the thunder and the lightning," the Great Spirit told Nasan. "Once the greatest of all giants, you are now the mightiest of all birds."

The Evening Star Lady was sent back to her place in the sky, and once more there was joy among the Indians.

Around the world Thunderbird now flies, the maker of the storm clouds and a wanderer of the dark skies. His voice is the noise of the thunder and the flash of lightning is the flapping of his wings.

Indian children do not fear the thunder or lightning, not even at night when it awakens them from their sleep. They know it is Nasan the giant, who became the Thunderbird.

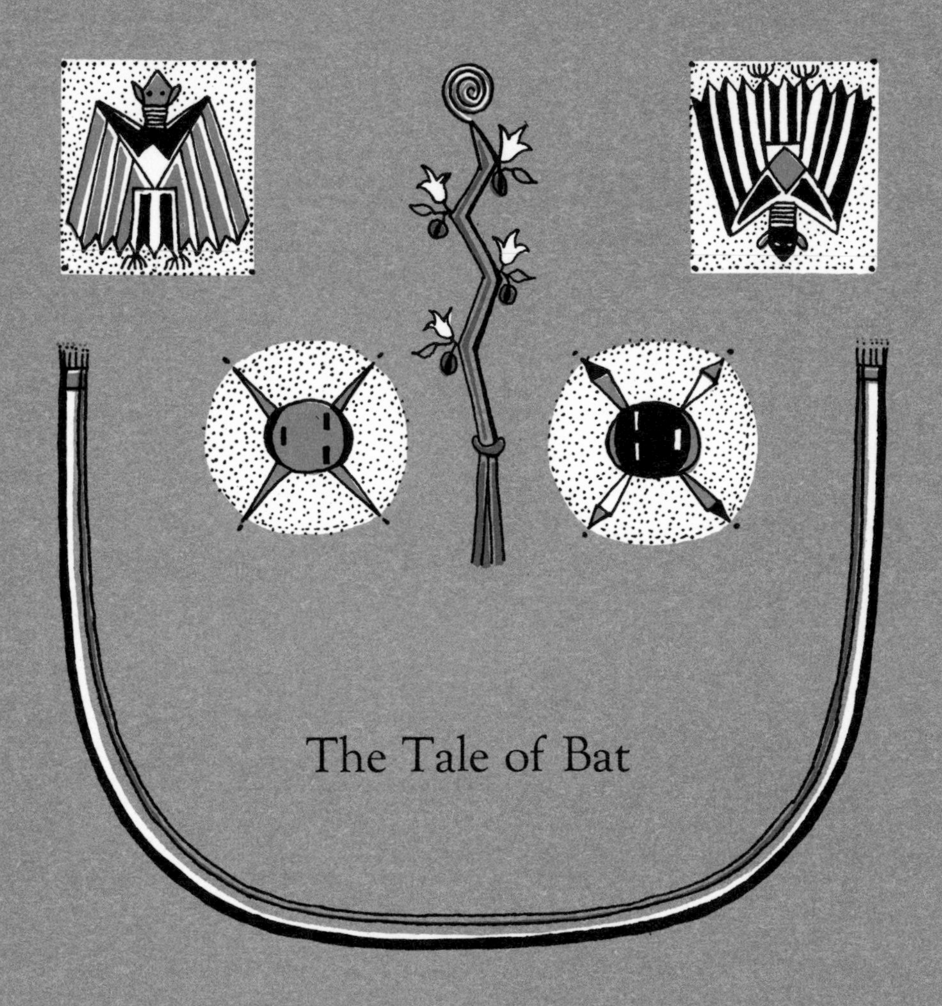

The Tale of Bat

When the earth was new, it all happened.

After the Great Spirit had fashioned the world, in the beginning of Indian Time, he raised the earth out of the water. But long before he brought the Red Man into the world, the Great Spirit made the earth a dwelling place for all animals, birds, and fishes.

The creatures of the air, the land, and the water lived together in harmony. The rabbit ran with the fox. The wolf and the wildcat dwelt together. The deer drank water in the same pool with the bear, and the buffalo cracked nuts with the squirrel. Snakes did not bite, nor wasps sting, and the eagle flew alongside the dove.

All the creatures — animals, birds, and fishes — spoke the same language. There was no confusion of tongues in the world in those days.

Unafraid, all the animals roamed the forest paths, the birds flew along the sky trails, and the fishes swam in their waters.

In this time every animal, bird, and fish in the land belonged to the same clan, and everybody called each other "Brother" or "Sister" or "Cousin." It was as simple as that, for the world was not so large then. Brothers, sisters, or cousins, everybody was happy. Truly, this was a wonderful time.

All the creatures could do *almost* anything they wished and they could go *almost* anywhere they liked. There was one place, however, where they could not go. The Great Spirit, ruler of the sky and creator of the world, had commanded them never to go down into the distant Valley of Flowers.

The greatest wonder of the land was the Valley of Flowers. More than sacred also was the Valley of Flowers.

Bright were the beams of the summer sun, and blue and clear was the long sky over the valley during the day.

Sacred was the valley even to the Wind Gods.

The North Wind never swept the cold over the valley, and the Storm Fool never danced here and threw snowflakes on the ground.

Here, the West Wind brought no fierce gales.

Here, the East Wind carried only gentle rain and the South Wind breathed soft breezes.

Here, in this sacred valley, were the precious seeds that the Earth Mother took to cover all the land with grasses, shrubs, trees, and the herbs and flowers that healed all sicknesses.

Beautiful was the valley, and more beautiful were the tens

of thousands of flowers and plants of all colors and scents that bloomed throughout the four seasons of the year.

Here were rare golden blossoms and strange-colored flowers that have never been seen since.

Here were the white flowers and purple-black fruit of the elderberry, the sweet honeysuckle blossoms, the fragrant juniper bushes, and the lovely redbud trees.

Here also grew the sacred flowers and plants. It was said that these plants had the bewitching powers of strong medicine, good medicine and bad medicine. And it was hinted, much grief and trouble would follow if they were destroyed or even picked by any except the careful hands of the spirit forms who lived in the unseen world.

In those days the Bat, who as you know has a little body and very large wings, flew in the daytime and slept during the night. Bat was a cheerful creature who loved to fly off a long way over the green fields and hills. One day he flew too far and came to the very edge of the forbidden Valley of Flowers.

Nervously fanning his enormous wings, little Bat flew high into the air and away from the Valley of Flowers. Bat did not stop flying until he was safely far, far away.

All the rest of that day, however, Bat thought of the Valley of Flowers.

He knew it was forbidden to enter it, but he was very curious. The more Bat thought about the valley, the more he longed to see it for himself; the more he wished to smell its beautiful flowers, and the more he yearned to taste the fruit and berries of the trees and sacred plants that grew in the valley.

The more Bat thought, the bolder he became.

Late that evening, while all the other creatures on earth were sleeping, Bat flew toward the forbidden valley. He reached it soon after dawn.

Noiselessly Bat flew down and slipped into the valley.

The morning breezes stopped dancing, and a hush fell over the land as Bat entered the valley.

Dazzling was the loveliness of the flowers that greeted Bat's eyes. Down close he came, to sniff every petal of each flower.

One flower smelled cool as a deep and quiet tree-shaded mountain pool. More fragrant than the honeysuckle was another flower. Fresh as the morning dew was another one. Fresher even than the freshness of a thousand summer evening breezes was yet another.

Bat found himself in front of a lily with the most graceful and slimmest of stems.

White the lily was; whiter than the blossoms of the plum tree; whiter even than the breast of the whitest swan. And fresh was its fragrance.

Suddenly, Bat had a craving for that lily. He wanted it more than anything else in the world.

Without further ado he plucked the petals of the lily and ate them. So good they tasted that he even ate the buds. And then he pulled the lily out of the ground.

Redder than the reddest of roses and foamy with bubbles was the juice that poured up out of the ground from the roots of the lily. It formed a pool at Bat's feet.

Bat bent down and tasted the red fluid.

Ten times sweeter than the honey of the bee it was, and more delicious than dewdrops warmed by the early sunbeams.

One taste tempted Bat to take another taste, and another taste, and then a sip.

Bat became overbold. Greedily he drank and drank. He rubbed some of the juice over his body. He dipped his wings in it. He even rolled in it. And then he drank of it again. Only when his stomach was full did Bat stop.

Bat did not know that the magic medicine of the Evil Spirits ran in the juice of the lily.

All the wicked noises of the world now hammered in Bat's head. And it was as if the mists of evening were before Bat's eyes, making him see all things in frightful shapes.

Bat tried to fly away, but he could not manage his wings.

It was even difficult for Bat to walk. All the world seemed upside down to him.

His little legs tangled with each other, and he tripped and crawled until he finally came out of the forbidden valley.

Bat was weary. He could not move any more. He covered his head with his wings and lay down to go to sleep.

Red-winged Blackbird, flying along the sky path, came down when he saw Bat lying on the ground with his wings covering his head.

"Are you ill, Cousin Bat?" he asked in a gentle whistle.

Bat took one wing away from his head, opened one beady little eye, and looked at Blackbird.

The most peculiar feeling in his head clouded Bat's mind with evil thoughts.

"Don't annoy me, foolish, fuzzy, noisy one!"

He screamed and he waved his wings violently at Blackbird.

Blackbird was so startled he could not click or whistle, and his feathers stood stiff on his body and wings.

It was the first time anybody had spoken so harshly to Blackbird. It was the first time anybody had ever told him he was foolish, fuzzy, and noisy.

Trembling and gasping for breath, Blackbird flew off in hasty flight to a nearby oak tree.

Blackbird sobbed. His pride was hurt, and anger was in his heart.

He threw down the largest acorn he could find at Bat.

Just then Fox came along, and the acorn fell on his head.

Fox saw Rabbit and thought that Rabbit had thrown the acorn at him.

Fox's face turned dark and angry. He snarled at Rabbit and struck him on the nose.

Rabbit hopped away in terror.

He had never been snarled at or struck by Fox before.

Snake, who was basking in the morning sun, was in frightened Rabbit's path.

Rabbit bared his teeth and screeched at Snake:

"Out of my way, lazy, ugly one!"

Rabbit kicked Snake aside.

Snake was by no means beautiful, and perhaps he was lazy. There was no reason, however, for Rabbit to say so. Neither was there reason for Rabbit to kick him. Rabbit's words were rude, his action most unkind.

"Big-eared monster!"

Snake hissed at Rabbit over his shoulder and glided off, zigzagging as fast as possible along the ground towards the safety of the pathless woods.

Harsh words, snarls, furious growls, bites, stings, scratches, and worse spread like a sickness from one creature to another in this once happy land.

All began to treat each other unkindly, and everybody made everybody else disagreeable. The most companionable of creatures were suddenly rude with one another, and quarrels were started over small matters. Before long, everybody was everybody else's enemy and life was no longer without peril.

No creature could tell what they feared, yet all were afraid.

The bigger animals rushed angrily through the woods and began to attack the smaller animals. All the four-footed ones

were afraid to run along the middle of the paths. Even Buffalo feared to move across the open fields.

The larger birds went on the warpath against the smaller birds, and all of the feathered ones, large and small, were afraid to fly too far or too high from their tree lodges.

All day long, until the Sun Chief went away and the Moon Man appeared in the sky, the birds, the beasts, and the other creatures trembled with fear and tried to keep out of sight of each other.

The leaves of the trees whispered of this trouble to the East Wind as he passed over the land the next morning.

Since nothing must be hidden from the Great Spirit, who was Father of the Sky and Creator of the Earth, the East Wind rose up to the edge of the sky and called out to the Great Spirit, who was in his lodge far above the clouds.

"Great Wisdom," cried the East Wind, "look down upon earth!"

The Great Spirit opened a hole in the floor of his lodge and looked down.

He saw that the birds did not sing from their tree lodges.

He saw the animals tremble with fear.

He saw the fish tribes cover their ears and hide their eyes.

He even heard little June Bug cry.

The Great Spirit saw all and knew all.

The Great Spirit, with his great magic, knew immediately that Bat had entered the forbidden valley and tasted and uprooted the wondrous white lily. He knew also that Bat had spoken the first unkind words, and that these words had led to more unkind talk and sowed the seeds of fear and trouble.

Great was the anger of the Great Spirit.

Down from the sky world to Bat's dwelling place on earth he came, on the back of a giant white eagle of incredible swift-

ness. So swiftly did this giant eagle fly that one could not even see his shadow.

The Great Spirit spoke.

"Bat," he said, "much mischief and misunderstanding have you caused."

Deep was the voice of the Great Spirit and stern were his words.

"You have done wrong and you have caused trouble and hate. It is my will that you be punished."

In silence Bat listened. He knew it was so. He had disobeyed the instructions of the Great Spirit. He had spoken evil. And he had caused others to do worse.

The Great Spirit looked upon Bat without pity. Sorrowful indeed was the trouble that Bat had caused. Sorrowful then must be his punishment.

"It is my will that you shall never again see the brightness of day," the Great Spirit told Bat.

"It is my will that forever and forever you shall move only in the night when paths are dark and lonely. You shall make your lodge only in gloomy caves and in the hidden branches of trees. In the daylight hours only shall you sleep. And always, when you rest or sleep, you shall hang by your feet with your head down in dishonor, and your wings shall cover your head in shame.

"I have spoken," said the Great Spirit.

Straightway the night opened and Bat disappeared into it.

So ends the tale of Bat as it is said to have happened in a time long, long ago. Always since, while the world sleeps and dreams at night, the bat flies. During the day he rests and sleeps, forlorn and motionless, with his head downward and his face covered by his large wings to hide his sorrow and his shame.

The Peace Pipe

When the earth was new, in the time of the very long ago, the Indians lived among each other in peace and plenty.

Manito, the Great Spirit, had made the land abundant and beautiful for the Red Men.

Blue was the sky and rich was the earth. The woods were filled with sweet wild berries and colorful flowers. Green were the grasses and tall were the trees in the hills and the valleys. The woods and the great forests were bountiful hunting grounds for deer, rabbits, and all sorts of other wild animals. Many also were the birds that lived and sang in the valleys and the forests. Cool were the waters that ran in the streams, lakes, and rivers, and all kinds of fishes swam in the waters of the land.

Each Indian tribe had their own dwelling place where they planted corn and tobacco. Every day they hunted wild animals or fished in waters that sparkled in the sun. Never did any Indian return empty-handed when he went out to hunt or fish. In the summer the Indians lived in wigwams. In the winter they lived in long cabins made of the bark of trees. There was enough on the land to give food and shelter to all men.

But there was jealousy among the tribes. Each wanted to hunt on the lands where other tribes made their lodges.

The Indians began to invade each other's hunting grounds. When braves of different tribes met on the trail, they glared angrily at each other.

"We hunt where we wish," said Indians who came from afar.

After a while the tribes began to shoot red painted arrows, a message of war, high in the air into the territory of their enemies. Soon, bands of warriors made raids against neighboring tribes. Then there was war all over the land.

In all the tribes the warriors painted their faces and bodies for battle. They chanted fighting songs and shouted terrible threats against their enemies as they held their wild and terrifying war dances.

"We are brave and not afraid," sang the warriors of one tribe, leaping high in the air.

"We are strong. We will take many scalps," the braves of another tribe boastfully sang out.

And the medicine men of the tribes waved their medicine bags and chanted prayers for victory.

Every Indian who could joined war parties. They rapped the trees with their war clubs as they followed their chiefs on the warpath.

Arrows were shot, tomahawks were raised, and knives were drawn as the tribes fought back and forth against each other.

Terrible were the war whoops, fierce was the fighting as each brave tried to take the scalps of his enemies. The more scalps, the more famous he might become. When the battles were over, the warriors returned home rejoicing over the defeat of their foes. The women, however, sang death songs as they wept for their husbands and sorrowed after their fathers and brothers who fell in the fighting and did not return.

After a while, the women did not smile proudly when their husbands and sons, brothers and lovers, went out on the warpath to face the weapons of their enemies.

Fairest among the young Indian maidens living then was Morning Flower, the daughter of the head chief of her tribe.

Tall and slender was Morning Flower. Fairer than the moon was her face. Her black hair was long and glossier than the feathers of the crow. Dark were her eyes; softer even than the eyes of a fawn they were. Truly, she was so beautiful that the tribal maker of songs sang about her loveliness.

Morning Flower worried each time her father, her brother, and even the handsome young braves who wished to win her for a wife went off to war. Already, many of the young braves she had known were lost in battle. The warpath might be the last path on earth for all those she knew and loved.

Each night Morning Flower prayed to the Great Spirit to turn all the Indian tribes from war back to the paths of peace.

Now, Morning Flower was no ordinary beautiful Indian girl, and her prayers were not ordinary prayers.

"O Great One!" she cried up to the sky. "You, who make

rain to water the land so all things on earth can grow, make our warriors put down their tomahawks, their war spears and shields. Turn their bows and arrows towards the hunt again. Make the trail straight and safe between all the tribes once more."

The all-wise Manito, the Great Spirit, who was Master of Life for the Red Men, watched the world from his lodge above the clouds. His heart was troubled as he beheld the signal fires of the war parties and the tribes fighting each other.

"Who will be left to pray to me if all fall in battle?" he wondered to himself.

The Great Spirit, who knew the acts of all men, looked down again on earth and heard Morning Flower's prayer.

"Surely," he said, "she has wisdom as well as beauty."

Down from his lodge in the sky to the earth, to Morning Flower's wigwam, came the Great Spirit.

When the night darkness curtained the earth and all were asleep, he came.

In the shape of a bright light, but unseen to all except in Morning Flower's dream, he came.

Three times the glowing light called, "Morning Flower . . . Morning Flower . . . Morning Flower."

In her dream Morning Flower looked up. She blinked her eyes as the bright light appeared before her.

"Morning Flower hears," she answered. "Who calls her?"

"The Great Unseen," replied the Great Spirit.

At once, even in her dream, Morning Flower bowed her head.

The Great Spirit's voice was stern as he spoke to Morning Flower.

"Tell your war chiefs to lay down their tomahawks and to paint their arrows white as a sign of peace," he commanded.

"This is not the proper task for a woman," said Morning Flower.

"If the braves wage war foolishly, a woman shall do what no wise man yet has done: call for peace," he told her.

Morning Flower bowed her head.

"Behold!" declared the Great Spirit. "I bring a sacred pipe. It is a gift to all the tribes."

In front of Morning Flower's blanket bed there suddenly appeared a pipe with a stem as long as her arm and a bowl that was deep enough to hold many fistfuls of tobacco. The stem was of a light wood painted with many beautiful colors, and eagle feathers were held to the stem by thongs of sacred deerskin. The bowl was made of a highly polished marble.

Round with wonder were Morning Flower's eyes when she beheld the sacred pipe.

"Most precious is this pipe," the unseen voice of the Great Spirit told Morning Flower.

"Why, O Great One?" asked Morning Flower.

"By it men shall know their friends," answered the unseen voice.

"How, O Great One?" asked Morning Flower.

"To offer the pipe to a stranger or an enemy at the council fire shall be a sign of friendship, a sign of peace," replied the Great Spirit.

"It will bring the tribes understanding," said Morning Flower.

"All men will think and talk their best thoughts when they smoke and pass this pipe around," the Great Spirit told her.

"It will turn the hearts of the war chiefs to peace," said Morning Flower.

"Truly, you have special wisdom," declared the Great

Spirit. "Heed what I have said," he warned her. "For you shall repeat my words to the medicine man and the chiefs of your tribe, and to the medicine men and the chiefs of all the tribes. I have spoken. No more will I say," said the unseen voice.

Suddenly, there was no bright light.

The Great Spirit vanished, and Morning Flower's dream was ended.

The beautiful and wise Indian maid awoke when morning came. She would not have believed her dream, had she not seen the sacred peace pipe beside her blankets.

Morning Flower woke her father, the chief.

"The Great Spirit came to me in a dream last night," she told her father.

She repeated to him the words the Great Spirit had spoken to her in her dream. And she pointed to the sacred pipe lying beside her sleeping blanket.

Her father listened to Morning Flower's words and looked at the sacred pipe.

Shaking his head in wonderment, he immediately went out and called together for a council meeting all the elders and all those who held positions of importance in the tribe.

"What is it that we have come to hear?" asked the medicine man. He spoke first, for he was the oldest of the tribe. Many, many were his years. His head was gray, dim were his eyes, and wrinkled was his face.

The chief looked proudly at his daughter who stood tall and graceful by his side.

"Morning Flower," he said, "has been called by the Great Spirit in a dream. She wishes to tell of the wisdom of the Great Spirit."

The old medicine man nodded his head.

"Let Morning Flower speak," he said. "All our thoughts shall be given to her words."

Morning Flower stepped forward and faced the tribal council.

"I speak the words of the Great Spirit," she said softly. "I will hide nothing."

They all bent forward and listened to Morning Flower's words.

"The heart of the Great Spirit is sad because all the tribes make war on their neighbors," she told them. "He has given us a sacred pipe of peace and friendship. He wishes the chiefs of all the tribes to be called to smoke this sacred pipe together. They will then talk out their quarrels, and they will again be as brothers in one family."

Morning Flower then told them all of the dream.

"This was the dream. Such were his words," she said when she had finished. "And this he has given us from the Sky World," she said, as she showed them the sacred pipe.

The elders and the chiefs of the tribe looked at Morning Flower with great respect. They stared at the pipe in deep awe.

The old medicine man rose to his feet.

"Morning Flower speaks the words of the Great Spirit, and the words are good," he said.

The old medicine man pointed to the pipe.

"All Indians should know of this great and sacred thing. Let us send messengers to every tribe to come together at a great council fire," he advised. "We will speak to each other from our hearts. We will smoke the sacred pipe together."

All those assembled in the tribal council nodded their heads in approval.

"Yes," agreed one of the elders of the tribe. "If we talk together with our enemies and smoke the sacred pipe with them, we shall take the path of peace together," he declared.

Messengers filled with speed were sent to all the tribes, asking them to come to a great council.

Swiftly they went at the rising of the sun, carrying white arrows as a sign of peace. Some went to the tribes in the nearby forests and the pleasant meadowlands. Many traveled along unknown trails for days and nights to bring word of the great council meeting to the tribes in the faraway hills and valleys.

Quickly around the land, by messenger and smoke signal, did the news spread of Morning Flower's dream and the Great Spirit's gift of the sacred Peace Pipe. The leaders and the wisest men of all the tribes listened to the messengers from Morning Flower's tribe. They agreed to come to the Great Council.

From far and wide to the council came the big chiefs and the great medicine men.

Without war paint they came.

Tall and erect and majestic, and with no fear showing on their bronzed faces, they came.

The chiefs came wearing plumed headdresses that trailed down their backs. The medicine men came carrying around their necks their medicine bags made of the skins of snakes and the feathers of birds. They kept their good medicine and magical charms in these bags.

Never before were so many great chiefs and medicine men gathered together at any council.

The chiefs exchanged gifts of buffalo robes, fine buckskin pouches, and wampum belts. The medicine men exchanged secrets of healing herbs.

Morning Flower's tribe held a dance of welcome for the

visitors. They made music with drums, gourds, and skin rattles.

All the medicine men began to fast and go into trances. They prayed and sought signs and visions that would help them make important decisions at the Great Council. Some medicine men drew magic circles and picture signs on the ground where they made their fasts.

Games and trials of skill and strength were held while the medicine men prayed and fasted. Many of the visiting chiefs made long speeches during this time.

Four days the medicine men fasted, and there were all sorts of signs of good medicine.

There was no rain the first day, but a rainbow hung high from one end of the horizon to the other.

On the second day, a plum tree blossomed in the morning and was full of plums by evening.

On the third day, wood that was burning under the cooking pots continued to burn even when one skin bag of water after another was thrown upon it.

On the fourth day, a very large white eagle feather floated down from the sky. No one had seen an eagle fly by, and no one had ever before seen an eagle's feather so white or so large. The feather fell on earth right in front of Morning Flower's wigwam.

The medicine men stopped their fasting and praying.

"Surely," said one of them, "these are signs of strong medicine from the Chief Above."

All the Indians rejoiced, and all the medicine men shook their snakeskin medicine bags in approval when the oldest of the medicine men lifted his hands and cried out:

"Gather wood and light the great fire! Bring forth the

ceremonial drums! Let all of us now take solemn council among ourselves!"

Logs and large and small branches of trees were gathered and heaped together for a great fire. At the going down of the sun the wood was lit.

Drummers beat the ceremonial drums of deerskin as the fire crackled and began to blaze. Soon it blazed higher and higher into the night, and all the chiefs and medicine men came and seated themselves in a wide circle around the fire.

They sat as equals around the fire: great chiefs from the big tribes, chiefs from the smaller tribes, famous medicine men and medicine men who were not well known. Behind them stood a large crowd of Indians.

The drums became silent when Morning Flower, dressed in her finest robe of the softest doeskin, came forward and stepped within the circle of the chiefs and medicine men.

By the light of the fire Morning Flower stood. All eyes were on her, for in her arms she carried the sacred pipe.

Morning Flower held up the sacred pipe. She spoke loud and clear:

"The Great One says that all Red Men shall have this pipe. They shall smoke this pipe together, and they shall prize peace as much as glory on the warpath. They shall live like brothers."

Translators spoke in sign language with their fingers, for many of the visiting Indians did not speak the same tongue as Morning Flower. However, all the Indians knew the sign language.

Morning Flower bent low and placed the pipe in the hands of the oldest of the medicine men. The honor of the first puff would be his.

The old medicine man rose to his feet. From the pouch around his neck in which he kept his good medicine, he took

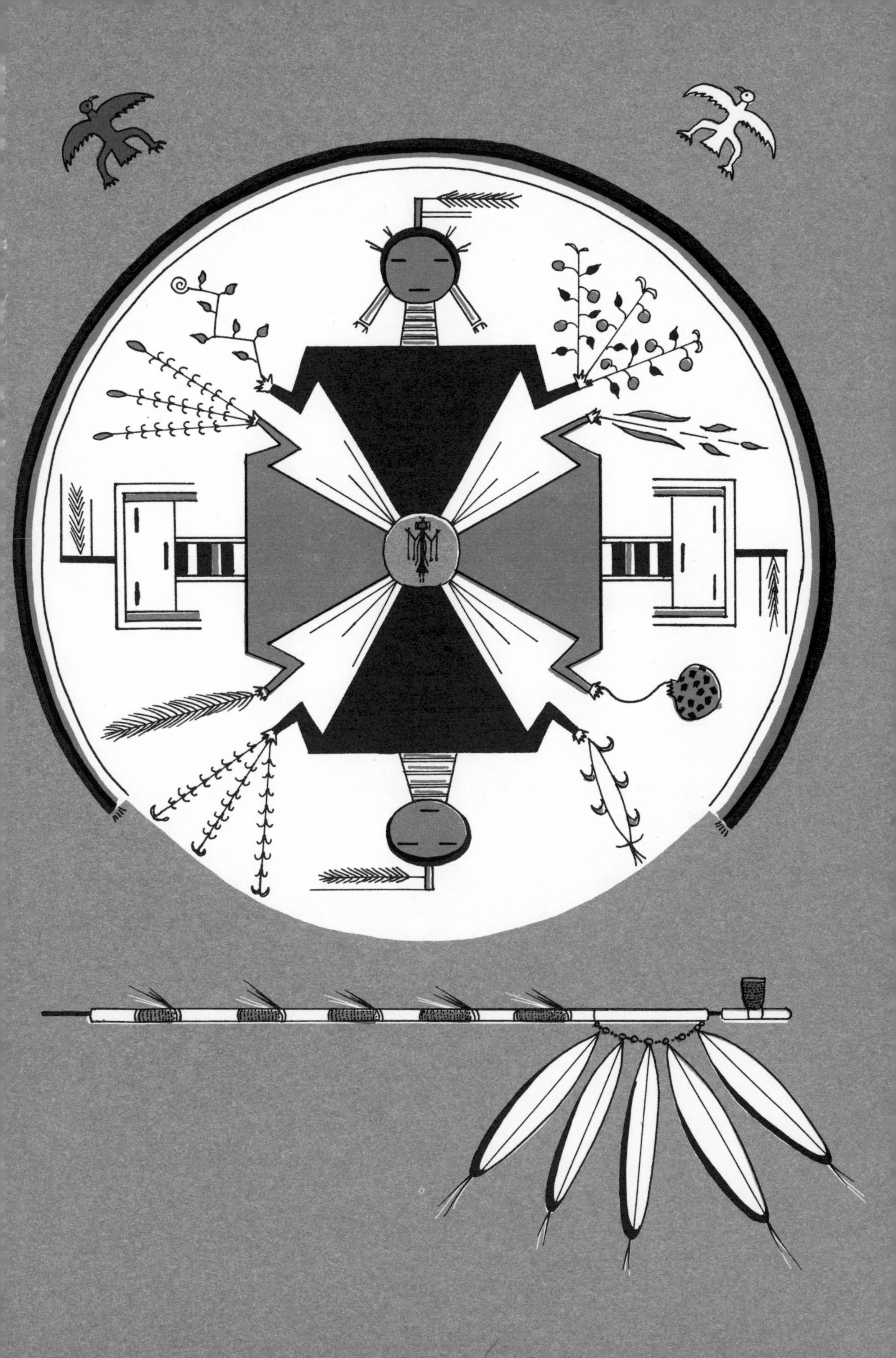

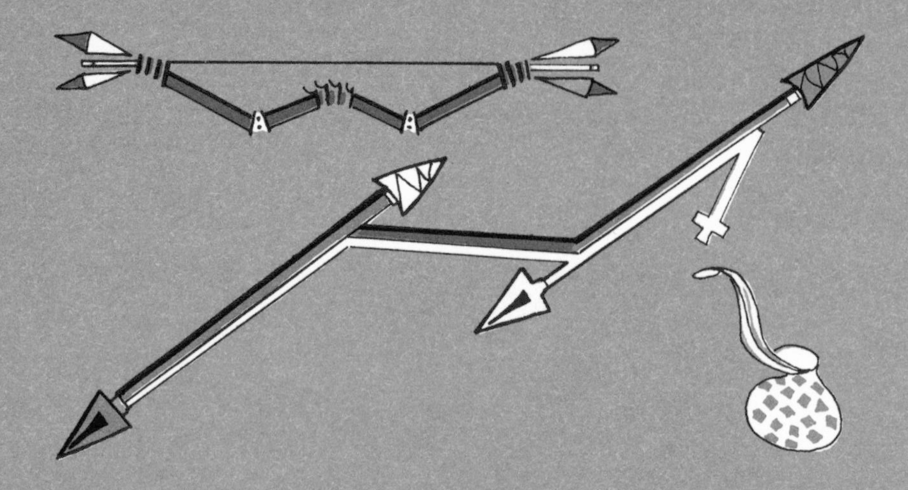

some sacred tobacco and filled the pipe with it.

With a small piece of burning wood from the great council fire, he lit the pipe.

He turned his face upwards and puffed at the pipe, blowing the smoke up towards the night sky.

Then he puffed and blew the smoke down towards the earth, and then towards the four major directions, north, east, south, and west.

"Let us make use of the Great One's gift," he said as he passed the sacred pipe to a mighty chief seated alongside him.

"Those who smoke the pipe together must live in peace with each other," declared the chief, and he took the pipe and puffed on it.

So, the sacred pipe was passed into the hands of all the chiefs and medicine men seated around the fire. And each of these Indians puffed on the pipe as it came into his hands.

"Let us obey the meaning of the pipe," said one medicine man.

"We will keep the peace we have pledged when we smoked the sacred pipe," declared one of the chiefs.

They all agreed to remember that those who smoke the pipe of peace together must not raise their weapons against each other.

"It is as the Great Spirit commands," said Morning Flower happily.

The drums began to beat again, and the Indians held a special dance in honor of the Peace Pipe and of the Great Spirit. They also held a special dance for Morning Flower.

A joyous feast followed and ended only when the first light of morning appeared in the sky.

The next day, when all the visiting chiefs and medicine men departed for their homes, they left as friends.

Thus, the Peace Pipe came to the Indians.

So, it became a law of peace and friendship for them.

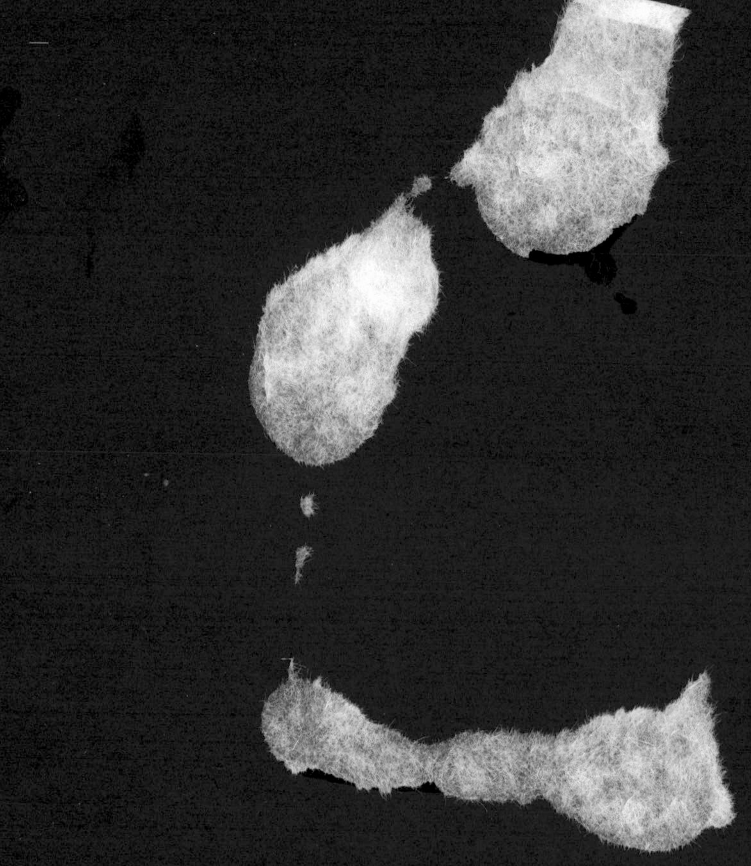